DREAMWORKS
Spirit
RIDING FREE

Lucky's Guide
to Wintertime Whimsy

Ellie Rose

New York Boston

Little, Brown and Company
Hachette Book Group
1290 Avenue of the Americas, New York, NY 10104
Visit us at LBYR.com
First Edition: October 2019

Little, Brown and Company is a division of Hachette Book Group, Inc. The Little, Brown name and logo are trademarks of Hachette Book Group, Inc.

The publisher is not responsible for websites (or their content) that are not owned by the publisher.

Library of Congress Control Number 2019932662

ISBN: 978-0-316-49095-5 (pbk.)

Printed in China

APS

10 9 8 7 6 5 4 3 2 1

OFFICIAL
MARK OF
SPIRIT

This book belongs to:

_____

Welcome, Winter!

Hi!

Long time, no see, friend! I almost didn't recognize you. That's probably because wintertime transforms <u>everything</u>—the way we dress, the way we take care of our horses, and even the way the whole world around us looks and feels. When it snows, it looks like everything is covered in sparkly diamonds, as Abigail might say!

I grew up in the big city. Every year, the trees that lined the sidewalks would lose their leaves and everyone would put candles in their windows. Each house glowed in a warm, beautiful way. Dad and I would make the

most of the chilly weather by going ice-skating in the park. Aunt Cora came, too, but would spend the whole time warning me not to go too fast....I didn't care. I loved the way my hair flew behind me in the wind. <u>Ah, memories!</u>

Winter is different here on the frontier. My two best PALs*, Pru and Abigail, grew up in Miradero and always talk about how winter really changes our usually hot and dry little town. During these months, the frontier can be even more untamed, wild, unpredictable, and exhilarating—kind of like my wild stallion, Spirit. Well, Spirit isn't really <u>mine</u>, but we're each other's in our own way.

In any case, you've come to the right place for some wintertime whimsy! I'm so excited to teach you how we celebrate in Miradero and to show you all the fun and ADVENTURE that comes with wintertime. Let's go!

You're a real frontier kid like me now, and it's going to be a wild ride.

*Just so you know, <u>PALs</u> is the nickname we use for the three of us: Pru-Abigail-Lucky. You can be our PAL, too!

Lucky

One thing that will never, ever change about wintertime—in the big city or the frontier—is that it's all about family. When it's chilly outside, snuggling up with your family, baking cookies, and singing songs is the perfect way to warm up. Of course, family can mean a lot of different things—parents, siblings, aunts, grandpas, and even friends, pets, and teachers.

My family has my dad; my stepmom, Kate; and my new sister, Polly.

Then there's Aunt Cora and Grandpa Prescott, as well as Fito and Estrella, who helped raise my mom, Milagro. They're pretty much my grandparents, just like Grandpa Prescott. I even like my cousin Julian... <u>sometimes.</u> And I could never forget Clancy, the very best Christmas goose, who came for dinner and never left!

Aunt Cora used to throw this big, fancy party in the city every year—the Winter Ball—to celebrate the season with our friends and family. It was the best! This year, she wants to celebrate with our friends and family here, so she's going to throw Miradero's first ever Winter Ball. Maybe we can help her later!

LUCKY

What's your favorite season?

In the city, I loved fall and spring the best
because of how the parks and streets would
change with the months. But in Miradero,
I really love winter and summer for exploring
the frontier! So, it's a tie!

What's your favorite thing about wintertime?

Either getting out to explore all the
changes on the frontier or staying in with
my family.

What's your favorite snow activity?

Sledding!

What's your favorite season?

_____

_____

_____

_____

_____

What's your favorite thing about wintertime?

_____

_____

What's your favorite snow activity?

_____

Spirit

Spirit has a special job throughout the winter. As the leader of Miradero's mustangs, he's in charge of making sure his wild herd is taken care of and that they have food, water, and shelter during the cold months. Sometimes my PALs and I give him extra help—like when we helped save a sick foal during a blizzard—but for the most part, he's got it under control.

When he's not out with his herd, Spirit spends time in the stable with Chica Linda and Boomerang, the other two best horses in Miradero. Here come Pru and Chica Linda now! I wonder what they think of winter.

Pru

Hiya, PAL! Glad you came to visit—though it's been especially snowy and cold this winter by frontier standards.

My whole life is about horses, and that doesn't change once it gets cold. My dad runs the biggest ramada (or ranch) in Miradero, maybe even on the whole frontier! In the winter, my dressage schedule slows down, which means I have time to help Dad on the ranch to keep the horses warm, clean, and healthy. And if they're not healthy, my mom steps in and fixes them right up. She's a vet!

What's your favorite season?

Don't tell anyone but...it's summer. Summer is when the best dressage events are held. PLUS, school's out, which means I have even more time to practice my riding.

Favorite winter family tradition?

Singing carols with my parents—but only inside the house where no one else can hear me!

During the winter, I love...

Making snow angels with my PALs!

Favorite winter family tradition?

During the winter, I love...

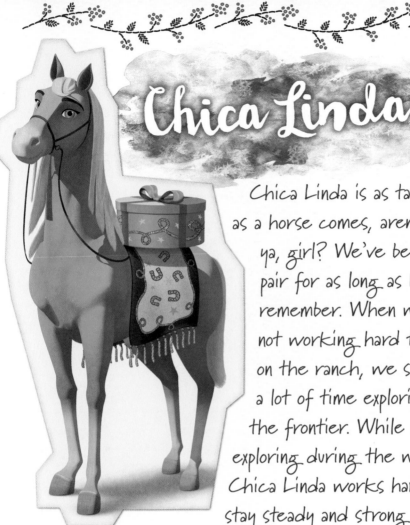

Chica Linda

Chica Linda is as talented as a horse comes, aren't ya, girl? We've been a pair for as long as I can remember. When we're not working hard together on the ranch, we spend a lot of time exploring the frontier. While we're exploring during the winter, Chica Linda works hard to stay steady and strong in the snow on the trails, and I work to make sure neither of us is too cold! Chica Linda loves when it's cold out— she likes kicking snow in the air to see it sparkle— but winter can be a difficult time for animals (and people!), so we gotta make sure that we're being safe and taking care of each other. But that's nothing new. Chica Linda and I know we can always rely on each other. I can't imagine getting through the winter—or ever—without her!

Abigail

You're here for winter! That's amazing! We can bake cookies and drink hot cocoa and make crafts and snuggle with Boomerang and have the Best Time Ever. I guess I do that kind of stuff most days... but it's all just better in the winter!

Winter is a nonstop thrill ride in Miradero—my PALs and I have saved girls from frozen lakes, ridden through blizzards, salvaged stranded train cars, and even overcome frontier flu!

The only bad part about wintertime is that when the weather gets ugly, I get stuck inside with Snips, my little brother. I guess he's okay sometimes, but for the most part he's a handful.... You'll see what I mean.

Abigail

11

What's your favorite season?

Winter! Wait, no, maybe it's summer? Scratch that—it's definitely spring...but who can forget about fall? I just love them all!

Favorite holiday treat?

Gingerbread for building, snickerdoodles for dunking in cocoa, and cinnamon rolls for dessert! Boomerang and I love licking icicles, too, even though my tongue sometimes gets stuck....

How do you spend a snowy day?

Building snow forts and getting into snowball fights with Snips!

Favorite holiday treat?

_____
_____
_____
_____
_____

How do you spend a snowy day?

_____
_____
_____
_____
_____

Boomerang

Now come on, you really need to meet Boomerang. He's pretty much exactly like me, except he's a horse (a pinto gelding to be exact!). Boomerang is the best horse to have around in the winter. He loves playing in the cold air and sliding down snowy hills with me. I spend a lot of time in the kitchen baking yummy wintry treats—and Boomerang loves trying them! He knows how to make the best of the weather, even when it's too chilly to be outside. He's happy to sit under a blanket with his pals—just like me! He's the most majestic steed in all the land!

Part 2
Don't Forget the Horses

Welcome to the barn! We end up spending a lot of our free time here throughout the winter. It's warm and cozy, but not <u>too</u> warm and cozy for our horses. We like to decorate it for Boomerang, Chica Linda, and Spirit, and we always bring a bunch of treats from Abigail's house for us all to enjoy.

We just have to make sure Boomerang doesn't eat all our fresh-baked cookies!

Let's get your horse set up with their very own stall in the barn, so we can all have fun together!

Don't have your own horse? Not a problem! Dreaming up a horse is half the fun. Trace a horse using this extra-special stencil, then cut out her or him to play along!

Wait—I just had the greatest idea! Instead of just _drawing_ your own horse, why don't you _bake_ one? I just found a gingerbread recipe that would be perfect. Once your horse is done, you can ice her or him to look just how you imagined. Here's the recipe:

Abigail

Gingerbread Horse

What You'll Need:

3 cups of flour, plus extra for dusting

1 teaspoon of baking soda

2 teaspoons of ground ginger

1 teaspoon of cinnamon

¼ teaspoon of salt

¾ cup of butter, softened

¾ cup of brown sugar

½ cup of molasses

1 egg

Horse stencil

Frosting, sprinkles, or any other cookie decorations!

Gingerbread Horse (cont)

What to Do:

1) Preheat the oven to 350 degrees. (Make sure an adult helps you with this part!)
2) Mix the flour, baking soda, ginger, cinnamon, and salt in a bowl.
3) Separately, use an electric mixer to beat the butter and brown sugar until it's fluffy. (An adult can help with this part, too!)
4) Add the molasses and egg to the butter and brown sugar, and mix until blended.
5) Slowly add the mixed dry ingredients to the wet ingredients until fully combined.
6) Flatten the dough with your hands and then refrigerate it until it's easy to shape, which should take about 30 minutes to an hour.
7) On a lightly floured surface, roll the dough with a rolling pin until it's about ⅛-inch thick.

8) Hold your stencil above the dough and use a sifter to lightly powder flour over the dough, so that you can clearly see the shape of your horse.

9) Cut the dough to match the horse, or get creative with its shape!

10) Move your cookies to a baking sheet and bake for 10 minutes, or until the edges are firm.

11) Allow to cool completely before frosting—then create whatever kind of horse you want!

Wow! Your horse looks ready to ride.
What will you name her or him?

_____

Spirit, Chica Linda, and Boomerang are so different! I bet your horse, _____, is unique, too. Take this quiz to find out which of our horses yours is most like!

LUCKY

1. While out on a winter ride, snow begins to fall unexpectedly. There's so much snow—it might be a blizzard! How does your horse react?

   A. Races off through the snow to make sure the rest of the herd has shelter.

   B. Heads home carefully and steadily. Riding in the fresh snow can be challenging, so precision and safety are key.

   C. Chases snowflakes with her or his tongue out! There's nothing yummier than fresh snow.

2. You've just made some cranberry and popcorn garlands to decorate the house. Your horse spots one of the garlands hanging in the living room through a window. What is your horse most likely to do?

   A. Walk right into the living room to inspect it more closely, even though your parents don't allow that!

   B. Scoff and keep walking. Humans do such silly things with their food!

   C. Somehow end up tangled in the garland. It looks fabulous.

3. You've been training all season long—what's your horse's favorite event?

   A. Trick riding

   B. Dressage

   C. Just clowning around!

4. It's a cold winter day and you and your horse just got back from a chilly ride! How does your horse warm up?

   A. Trick question! Your horse is used to spending her or his time outside and doesn't need to warm up.

   B. Settles into the barn with a blanket to rest.

   C. Eats, eats, eats!

5. The PALs just built the most beautiful, elaborate snowman in all Miradero. Well, technically, it's a snow horse. How does your horse react when he or she sees it?

   A. Gives it a suspicious sniff, then walks away.

   B. Doesn't pay it much attention. It's just a pile of snow, after all!

   C. Eats its carrot nose. Whoops!

If you chose mostly As...your horse is most like Spirit!
Your horse is independent and doesn't always like being told what to do, but will always be there for you.

If you chose mostly Bs...your horse is most like Chica Linda!
Your horse is disciplined and works hard to make you proud. Together, you strive for perfection and make an unstoppable team!

If you chose mostly Cs...your horse is most like Boomerang!
Your horse always wants to make you smile. You're both goofy and don't take yourselves too seriously, but you know deep down that there is no nobler horse-and-rider pair in the world!

Gingerbread Horse Treats

Boomerang! Do not eat our new gingerbread horse friends. They are majestic steeds and...oh. Lucky, these gingerbread horses are delicious.

Mmm, maybe we can distract Boomerang with some tasty gingerbread treats just for horses. Abigail, why don't you help me? I think you need the distraction, too....

Want to make a special version for _your_ animal pals? Don't fret—it's the Granger family's secret recipe to the rescue! I know plenty of animals that will love it: horses, puppies—

Donkeys, too?!

Yes, Snips. Donkeys, too!

Gingerbread Horse Treats

What You'll Need:

- 1-½ cups of flour
- 1 tablespoon of ground ginger
- ½ teaspoon of ground cinnamon
- ¼ teaspoon of ground cloves
- ¼ cup of molasses
- ¼ cup of water
- 2 tablespoons of vegetable oil

What to Do:

1) Preheat the oven to 325 degrees. (Make sure an adult helps you with this part!)
2) Mix the flour, ginger, cinnamon, and cloves together.
3) Whisk the molasses, water, and vegetable oil in a separate bowl.
4) Mix the dry ingredients into the liquid mixture until well combined.
5) Roll out the dough with a rolling pin until it's about ¼-inch thick.
6) Using cookie cutters, cut treats in the shapes of your animal friend's favorite things as a special surprise!
7) Move your treats to a baking sheet, bake for 20 minutes, and cool completely before serving.
8) Share them with your pet and see how happy she or he is!

Boomerang! Those hadn't cooled yet....Oh well.

Wintertime Horse Care

Now that you have your own horse, you should learn how to take care of her or him in these cold, blustery months. And where better to learn than my dad's ranch? Look, there's my dad and Turo, the blacksmith's apprentice, now! What can you two tell us about taking care of a horse in the winter? **PRU**

Well, just as people like to wear warm socks and hats, drink homemade soup, and sit by the fireplace when it's cold out, horses also need special care during the winter. **TURO**

That's right. On the ranch, we work hard to make sure these horses are just as healthy during these cold frontier winters as they are in the summers. Remember, horses are built for winter. They're usually warmer than we are!

Here are some tips for taking care of your horse on cold days:

* Give him or her warmed water.
* Feed him or her extra hay.
* Bring him or her inside the barn whenever it gets too cold.
* Keep him or her nice and dry.
* Spend extra time with your horse to make sure he or she is behaving normally.

Spirit doesn't like to be cooped up, but no horse can say no to a warm barn. With some decorations, it feels just like home! How would you make this stall feel like home for your horse, _____, in the winter?

LUCKY

Do Horses Get Cold in Winter?

Horses start growing winter coats at the end of summer or in early fall, depending on where they live. Their bodies can sense when it's getting cold, and they start growing long, thick hair that keeps them cozy all winter long. Sometimes it even grows in fluffy instead of flat to trap more warmth. Since they can't go buy a new coat at the general store, nature kicks in instead!

Did you know that horses are supposed to graze all the time? Their constant digestion of food keeps them warm. So, in the winter, they might want to graze even more, which produces more body heat.

Who knew? Hair and snacks are the secrets to staying warm!

What About Hair Clipping?

Do you ever get a new haircut during the winter to celebrate the changing of the seasons? Horses get their hair clipped in the winter, too, but for different reasons!

Caretakers clip unique patterns into their steeds' coats to help them regulate their body temperature. If the horses are working hard on the ranch, they might sweat a whole lot, and having clipped hair helps the sweat cool them down. Then caretakers balance things out by covering them with blankets to keep them warm. It's kind of like wearing a hat!

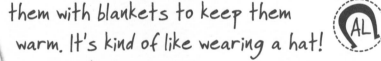

That's right, Dad! Sometimes we clip our horses' hair with a simple stripe right down their belly. It's discreet and easy! But the most interesting horse clippings I've ever seen were on Lucky's friend Mixtli's horse, Crow. Just take a look at them!

If you decided to clip the hair on your horse,
_____, what would it look like?

Design Your Own Horse Blanket

One of the best parts about winter is giving gifts. My favorite gift to give Boomerang is a brand-new blanket, made with love by _me_.

Trace the blanket below onto a separate piece of paper. Make your own special design for your horse, _____. Then you can cut it out and fold along the line so your horse can wear it all winter long!

Abigail

Trail Riding

Chica Linda and I love getting out on the trail, racing through the snow, and feeling the chilly wind against our faces. Don't we, girl? Leaping over snow drifts, whooshing past bear caves, and galloping around icy lakes is thrilling and takes a lot of skill. It even took Lucky a while before she mastered the new frontier terrain. You and your horse, _____, should give winter riding a try with these obstacles! Punch them out and set up a course of your own!

PRU

Winter Gear

You know what's important for winter riding? Your boots! The right boots will keep your toes warm. Warm toes mean safer, more controlled riding. Make sure your gear is always in good shape and doing its job!

You know what else is important?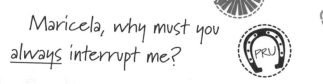

Maricela, why must you <u>always</u> interrupt me?

I'm just trying to help you girls! Plus, as the mayor's daughter, it's my duty to introduce all our friends to the ins and outs of Miradero, no matter what the season. By the by, the answer is <u>staying fashionable</u>.

Ugh, that is <u>not</u> that important!

Nonsense! Personal expression and being true to yourself is the <u>most</u> important. You girls taught me that!

That's actually pretty nice....Okay. Go ahead.

Design Your Own Fashionable Winter Boots!

A good pair of boots can be functional _and_ fashionable. They can set you apart from other riders and express who you really are! What would _your_ riding boots look like?

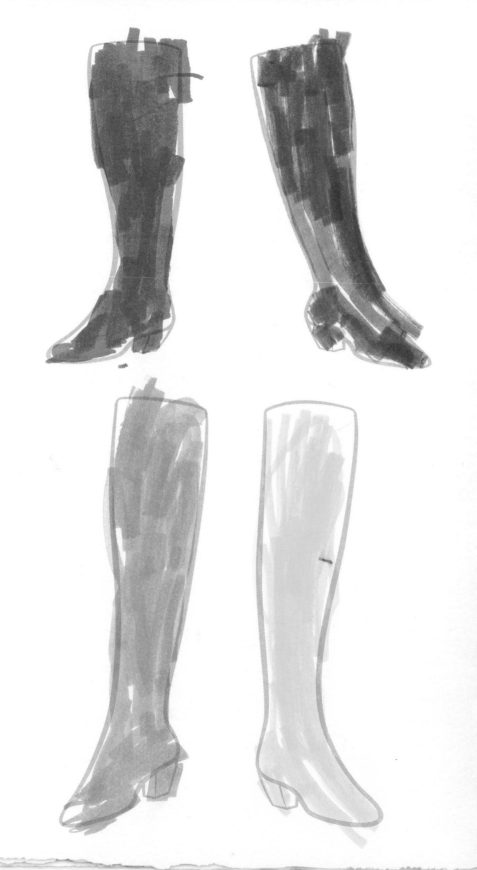

This is Miradero's inn, where my aunt Cora lives! Today's an important day—as Aunt Cora keeps reminding me—because tonight she's throwing Miradero's first ever Winter Ball! **LUCKY**

Miss Prescott is a teensy bit stressed out. **Abigail**

I get why. <u>It's stressful.</u> The whole town is talking about this party, and there's still so much to do. **PRU**

Oh, all my favorite young ladies have finally arrived! I've decided to stay calm today, no matter what, so I'm not even a bit upset that you are seven and a half minutes late. Everything is going wrong, but <u>it is going to be fine.</u> **Cora**

That vein in her forehead is poking out again.... **PRU**

What's going on, Aunt Cora?

We're finally going to be able to celebrate my favorite season in style. I'm going to transform this inn from the roof down to the floorboards. Wreaths and snowflakes and cookies galore! Can't you just see it now? **Cora**

Am I the only one who doesn't see any decorations? Are they invisible? *Abigail*

I haven't had time to decorate because I'm too busy worrying! There's a blizzard on its way, and a train carrying treats for the party is supposed to come into town tonight! What if the train gets caught in the storm and the treats never make it? How can you have a Winter Ball without treats?! **Cora**

Don't worry, Aunt Cora. We can help you out with the decorating part! We'll play the new Sally Jessup record and get this place wonderlandified in no time. And Spirit will help, too, won't you, boy? LUCKY

I was doing my best to ignore that Spirit had followed you into the foyer. But okay—thank you, girls. I have a list of decorations to make right here. Why don't you get started? **Cora**

Winter Crafts

The easiest way to make a space look festive and ready for the holidays is with a garland! The best thing about garlands is that you can make them with just about anything, like popcorn or cranberries or plenty of other things you might have around the house! Here's a fun one to get you started.

Pinecone Garland

What You'll Need:
- Twine
- Pinecones
- Scissors
- Extra yarn, ribbons, or tree ornaments!

What to Do:

1) First things first: time to go outside and find some pinecones! If you don't live near pine trees, you can buy some at a local craft store.

2) Have an adult help you cut a long piece of twine. If you're measuring the garland for a particular spot, remember to cut the twine extra long. The pinecones will weigh it down and take up space.

3) Lay out all your materials.

4) Take a pinecone, wrap the twine under a layer of scales toward the top, and knot it. The twine will be hidden inside the pinecone.

5) Repeat Step 4 with another pinecone next to the first one! Keep linking pinecones and twine until your garland is filled.

6) If you have spare yarn, ribbons, or even tree ornaments, you can fill the spaces between the pinecones for an extra-festive garland. I like to add big red bows to mine!

Even though a storm is brewing outside, there isn't nearly enough snow _inside_ to make this a real winter wonderland. Why don't we make some?! Okay, so it's not icy or yummy on the tip of your tongue like _real_ snow, but this "snow" does _look_ and _feel_ pretty real. You can use it to make a perfect winter scene for your horses!

Abigail

Year-Round Snow

What You'll Need:

Baking Soda

1 cup of baking soda
Shaving cream

What to Do:

1) It's so easy! Get a big bowl and pour in the baking soda. Slowly add shaving cream, and mix with your hands until it feels like snow.

There's nothing as special as catching snowflakes on your fingertips! It's so fun to see the patterns of the flakes and how each one is so different from the others. I always wish that I could keep the snowflakes forever, and with this craft, you actually can!

LUCKY

3-D Snowflakes

What You'll Need:

Scissors
Square-shaped paper

Tape
Stapler

String

What to Do:

1) Fold a piece of square paper in half, corner to corner, to create a triangle.

2) Fold the triangle in half again, from corner to corner, to make a smaller triangle.

3) Have an adult help you cut three lines from the the first fold you'd made in your paper across the triangle, one on top of the other. The lines should be parallel to the bottom of your triangle, or the longest edge. Be sure not to cut the entire way across!

4) Now unfold your paper. Your square should look like it has four arrows pointing toward opposite corners on each half of the paper.

3-D Snowflakes (cont)

5) Take the innermost arrows in the middle of your square and roll them together to make a tube. Tape them together like that!

6) Flip over your paper. Roll the next two arrows together to make another tube and tape them together.

7) Flip your paper back to the original side and roll the next two arrows to make a tube and tape them together.

8) Flip your paper one more time and roll your final two outermost arrows together to make a tube and tape them together. Your original square should now look like a diamond-shaped twist!

9) Repeat Steps 1-8 five more times. You should have six twists in total.

10) Have an adult help you staple one end of each of the twists all together to form a snowflake shape. You can then staple the middle of the twists to each of the twists next to them to make sure your snowflake shape stays in place!

11) Wrap some string around the center of the snowflake to hang it up, creating your own winter wonderland!

The Fun of Gift Giving

Lucky, Tanglefoot Inn looks positively beautiful. It's the winter wonderland of my dreams! But outside is looking snowier than I'd have hoped. There's no way the train will be able to make it through this blizzard. We won't be able to have the special treats I'd planned!

Cora

Then Spirit and I will ride out to the train line and gallop through the snow until we find that delayed train, and <u>save the day</u>! Spirit's the fastest horse around—we'll be back in a jiff!

LUCKY

YEAH! PRU

Yeah?

Abigail

Absolutely not. The train probably stationed at the last stop in the town of Silverlode to wait out the storm, anyway. The train is safe, and you should be, too. It's just my surprise that's a lost cause.

Cora

I guess you're right. But there must be a way that we can still make the party extra special!

Hmm....What if we ask everyone what their favorite things are and bring those to the party? Boomerang can help us get to everyone fast enough!

Chica Linda, too! Right, girl?

Well, I suppose that could work. Thank you, girls. That's a kind gesture, and I'm sure our guests will appreciate it!

WE'RE ON IT!

Visit Jim, Kate, and Polly

First stop: my house!

My dad, my stepmom, and I spent a whole day decorating our home for the season. We have candles and wreaths and winter flowers everywhere. Sometimes Spirit likes to nibble on them, but Kate's <u>mostly</u> used to that now.

This year, I wanted to make sure the winter was perfect for my new sister, Polly. She's still a baby, but I think she really likes it. I can't wait for her to grow up and have her very own wild horse like Spirit!

LUCKY

Welcome home, Lucky!

Doesn't the snow look beautiful?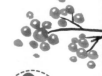
Polly is mesmerized by the snowflakes.

That's why we're here! The snow is holding up a
train with Aunt Cora's special Winter Ball surprise
in Silverlode, so we want to come up with something
equally special to make up for it.

Is that so? Hmm...

Have you thought about hosting a Secret
Snowflake? That's what we did in the orphanage
when I was growing up.

How can we do that?

Secret Snowflake

We all wanted to give all our friends extra-special gifts, but sometimes there wasn't enough time to do that. So instead, we'd write everyone's names on pieces of paper, then fold the papers and put them in a hat. Everyone pulled a name out of the hat and would find just the right gift for the person they picked. Different groups can agree on what kind of present everyone should get. Should everyone spend five dollars, or make the gift by hand? Should they be silly or charitable? After everyone got their gifts, we would gather together to exchange, and each person tried to guess who their secret snowflake was! The best part of Secret Snowflake is that everyone gets to give <u>and</u> receive a gift specially picked for her or him, each unique like a snowflake.

You can try this with your friends!

Kate

Visit Maricela

Hi, Maricela! LUCKY

Welcome, Lucky and friends! And your smellier, four-legged friends I've grown to accept. How can I help you on this snowy day?

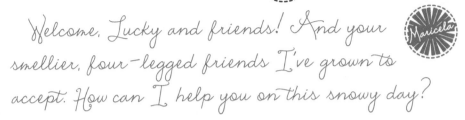

We're figuring out what our friends and family love the most about winter, for no reason in particular. What do you like to do? LUCKY

As the First Daughter of Miradero, I'm always busy spreading joy and happiness to my constituents throughout the winter. I perform traditional songs; I hand deliver gift baskets; I remind my fellow PALMs how fortunate they are to have me...ahem, I mean, one another. It's a full-time job making sure every home in Miradero has its share of joy. But sometimes, a simple card can bring joy to a friend down the street or even one across the world.

Help me spread joy by decorating these postcards for your friends!

Add a note, address, and stamp.
Then drop it in the mail.

Message:

stamp
here

To:

_____

_____

_____

_____

_____

Address

From:

Message:

stamp
here

To:

_____

_____

_____

_____

_____

Address

From:

Lucky...may I confide in you, as a close, personal friend?

Um, sure. What's winter about if not friendship?

Well, my father, the mayor, buys me so many wonderful gifts and I adore him for it, but...I wish someone would make something special just for me. You know, a handmade present, like you all love to get.

You want a handmade gift?

You make them seem so special!

Hmm...I have a feeling Aunt Cora's Winter Ball will have something special for you, too.

Oh! Do you really think so, Lucky?!

Lucky's Very Special
Fashion Scarf for Maricela

What You'll Need:

Yarn   Scissors

What to Do:

1) Unravel the start of a ball of yarn and hold the end down with the thumb of your nondominant hand with your palm facing up.

2) Using your dominant hand, weave the rest of the yarn around the fingers of the hand holding the yarn, starting behind your index finger, then in front of your middle finger, then behind your ring finger, and finally in front of your pinky.

3) Loop back around your pinky finger and weave back in the opposite direction to your index finger.

4) Loop around your index finger and weave between your fingers again like you did in Step 2 to end on your pinky. You should now have two loops of yarn on each finger.

5) With your palm still facing up, carefully take the bottom loop of yarn on your index finger and lift it over the tip of your finger, passing over the top loop of yarn. Repeat this on your other fingers. That's row one!

6) Now repeat Steps 2–4 so that you're back to having two loops of yarn on each finger, then repeat the looping from Step 5!

7) Once your scarf has reached your desired length, stop twisting yarn around your fingers so that you're left with only one loop of yarn. Take the loop from your pointer finger up and over your middle finger so that you have two loops on your middle finger. Take the bottom loop of yarn and lift it over the tip of your finger as you did in Step 5. Repeat this step with your ring finger and pinkie.

back

8) Carefully take your final loop off your pinkie! Take the end of your yarn, push it through that loop, and pull it tight.

Visit Snips

Welcome to my home, where the scent of freshly baked pies and jam cooking are always in the air! That is, unless my little brother, Snips, ate everything....Speaking of which, where _is_ Snips?

I'm right here, but it doesn't matter. Señor Carrots and I don't wanna see anybody right now.

Oh well! I suppose we should just move on, then. BYE, SNIPS!

Abigail...

Fine. Snips, what's wrong?

UGH. It's the <u>snow</u>! I thought it would be fun, but it's just <u>cold</u>. My toes are frozen, Señor Carrots got his tongue stuck to an icicle, and, for some reason, nobody will give me ice cream! It's the worst time of year.

Would some ice cream make you feel better? Because that gives me an idea....

We can give Snips this recipe for making ice cream out of snow!

Abigail

Snips's Snow Ice Cream

What You'll Need:

8 big cups of freshly fallen snow
   (or shaved ice)
½ can of evaporated milk
½ can of condensed milk
1 teaspoon of vanilla
1 teaspoon of maple syrup
Your favorite toppings!

What to Do:

1) In a big bowl, mix the evaporated milk, condensed milk, vanilla, and maple syrup.
2) Once it's combined, fold the mixture into your snow bit by bit until you have the right consistency for your ice cream.
3) Snow can be soft and fluffy, or heavy and icy, so taste test as you go to get it just right!
4) When you're happy with your ice cream, add your favorite toppings!

Visit Turo

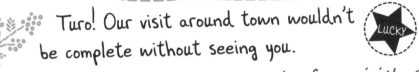

Turo! Our visit around town wouldn't be complete without seeing you. LUCKY

Oh, I always like when you stop by for a visit! I heard a rumor that you and your friends are collecting presents for the townsfolk. Is that true? TURO

You caught us! PRU

Oh no! Is the surprise ruined? Abigail

Not at all! But don't worry about me. I don't need anything! I like spending time with everyone. Isn't that the best gift of all? TURO

You're so right, Turo. The Winter Ball tonight will be a hit no matter what, because we'll all be there together. Thanks for reminding us. LUCKY

But you don't want <u>anything</u>? PRU

How about a picture together, so I can always remember having fun with my friends this winter? Right here is perfect, with all my friends and our horses. TURO

That's a great idea, Turo! LUCKY

Now, say <u>cheese</u>!
Draw a festive picture of you and
your friends in the frame below!

Now that we have all our presents finished, we should head back to the barn and get ready for the Winter Ball! Spirit needs to go check on his herd, anyway. **LUCKY**

That means it's time for the best part of all: wrapping! I've got folding the paper down to an exact science. It's all about precision, measurements, and— **PRU**

RIBBONS. It's all about the ribbons. *Abigail*

Actually, yeah. Ribbons are important, too! **PRU**

I wanna peek! **SNIPS**

Don't you want a special *Abigail* *surprise to unwrap at the party?* I've decided I don't wanna peek! **SNIPS**

How to Wrap a Present

What You'll Need:

Wrapping paper　　　Tape
Scissors　　　　　　Ribbons

What to Do:

1) On a flat surface, lay out your wrapping paper. Place your gift box, bottom side up, in the middle of the paper. Wrap the edges of the paper around your gift, from the left and the right, and the top and the bottom, to make sure it will cover about half of the

box from each side. Move your gift around to get the length just right from every angle! Once you do that, add a few extra inches to the length of paper you just measured. That's how much paper you need.

2) Have an adult help you cut your measured length of paper.

3) Now re-center your box on the cut paper. Wrap the left side up so it meets the center of the bottom of your box. Secure it with a small piece of tape.

4) Pull the right side of your paper up and over the edge you just secured, and tape this side down as well. The top and bottom of your gift should still have paper sticking out.

5) Now it's time to make the flaps! Push both ends of the paper inward to the bottom of the box.

6) Fold the corners of your flattened paper in toward your gift to make two small triangles.

7) Take the flap you just made and fold it up against your gift box. Tape down the end!

8) Repeat Steps 5-7 with the top side of your gift!

9) Flip over your wrapped present and top it off with a bow or ribbons! Don't forget to add a name tag or card.

Thank You

Can you believe we really did it? We made and wrapped all these gifts in time for the Winter Ball. Aunt Cora is going to be so happy!

LUCKY

It's a winter miracle!

PRU

And we couldn't have done it without you, friend!

Abigail

To say thank you for all your help, we made you a little gift. We hope you like it!

LUCKY

Thank You

The Best Gift in the World is Friendship

Part 4
A Winter Adventure

We need to get all our gifts over to the party. Boomerang, Chica Linda...I know Aunt Cora won't want you <u>inside</u> the inn during the Ball, but maybe you can help us deliver the presents? I have a feeling that there are a few specially wrapped bran mashes in there just for you both! LUCKY

With the snow coming down so hard, I think we'll need to get out the sleigh. I don't think we'll make it to Tanglefoot Inn from the barn otherwise! PRU

Don't worry—Boomerang was born for this. Abigail

57

Oh no! The blizzard is way worse than we thought. We'll never get to the Inn, even with a sleigh! What are we going to <u>do</u>? The Winter Ball starts in an hour, and we're stuck here with the surprises for everyone! I can't believe we're going to let down Aunt Cora.

Stay calm. I'm sure there's a way out of this barn. We just need to think rationally.

Maybe if we sing at the top of our lungs we can cause an avalanche that will set us free! Boomerang can help. SING, BOOMERANG, SING!

... LUCKY ... PRU

Why don't we come up with a plan B? You know...in case that doesn't work.

If you say so, but I'm sure we won't need it!

PALs, we need to bust out of here. If only we could get past the snow blocking the barn door...

That snow outside is too dangerous. If we try and dig our way out, we might just end up making it worse—or getting frostbite. We need to get a signal out to get someone's attention.

You're all wrong. I'm a real adventurer, and I'm gonna save us!

SNIPS! What are you doing here?

I followed you, DUH. I saw you guys having fun with all the presents, and I've got the right to fun, too!

Yeah, let him have fun and presents!

Ugh, I tried to stop this.

Don't you worry, ladies. Señor Carrots and I have the best plan EVER.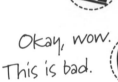

Okay, wow. This is bad.

We have to figure out a way to make it to the Winter Ball! PAL, what would you do?

To try LUCKY'S PLAN, go to page 61.

To try PRU'S PLAN, go to page 62.

To try ABIGAIL'S PLAN, go to page 64.

To find out what SNIPS, BIANCA, and MARY PAT have in mind, go to page 69.

Lucky's Plan

"Okay!" says Lucky. "We have no time to lose. We've got to get the barn door open so Spirit can help us."

Lucky tells Abigail to gather as many wooden tools as she can find and tells Pru to grab some rope. She bundles the tools together and quickly ties the ropes around them in a series of elaborate knots to bind them together. She's made a battering ram!

"Everyone, grab on! We're going to slam this into the door. Maybe we can push the door hard enough to move the snow out of the way. Now, CHARGE!"

As Chica Linda and Boomerang eye the battering ram warily, everyone takes hold of it. Lucky counts to three, and you and the rest of your friends charge the door. It doesn't budge.

What should you do next?

To convince Chica Linda and Boomerang to help, go to page 67.

To try the battering ram again, go to page 68.

To try another plan, go back to page 60.

Pru's Plan

"All right, Lucky. I'm going to need your help," Pru says, turning to her friend with determination. "You still remember your trick riding training?"

"Javier and I practice every time he's in town," Lucky responds. "I'm a <u>pro</u>. But how will that get us out of here?"

Pru looks up, past the rafters, at the untended hole in the roof. It was her job to patch it, but she hasn't gotten to it just yet.... Now it is going to help them escape. Lucky just needs to balance on Chica Linda's back with Pru on her shoulders. Then Pru will be able to crawl through the hole with a lantern and flash its light to get someone's attention!

"Are you sure you can do <u>all that</u>?" question Bianca and Mary Pat in unison.

"Yes! I'm sure this will work!"

Lucky nervously hops onto Chica Linda's back. The horse holds steady and sure. Once she's up, Lucky reaches her hand out to Pru.

With you, Abigail, and Boomerang helping lift her, Pru makes it to Lucky's shoulders and just as swiftly jumps to the hole in the roof.

SNAP!

"NO!" Pru cries.

The wood of the roof cracks some more. It really needs replacing—and now Pru is hanging by four fingers from a wooden beam a long way from the ground.

"You should come <u>down</u>, Pru!" Abigail says anxiously. "I'll try to catch you!"

"Ah!" Pru wavers, but she adjusts her fingers and gets a better grip. "Don't worry! I can do this!"

"What should we do?" Lucky calls.

To try another plan, go back to page 60.

To have Pru stick to her plan, go to page 71.

Abigail's Plan

"You've made the **right** choice. Now, sing!"

Dashing through the snow
In a one-horse open sleigh
O'er the fields we go,
Laughing all the way.

Bells on bobtail ring,
Making spirits bright.
What fun it is to ride and sing
A sleighing song tonight!

Jingle bells, jingle bells,
Jingle all the way.
Oh! what fun it is to ride
In a one-horse open sleigh.

Jingle bells, jingle bells,
Jingle all the way.
Oh! what fun it is to ride
In a one-horse open sleigh.

A day or two ago,
I thought I'd take a ride,
And soon Miss Fanny Bright
Was seated by my side.

The horse was lean and lank.
Misfortune seemed his lot.
He got into a drifted bank,
And then we got upsot!

Jingle bells, jingle bells,
Jingle all the way.
Oh! what fun it is to ride
In a one-horse open sleigh.

Jingle bells, jingle bells,
Jingle all the way.
Oh! what fun it is to ride
In a one-horse open sleigh!

The ground starts to shake...or is that the walls? Boomerang neighs worriedly. He hides in the corner with Snips, who then jumps into a pile of hay, followed by Bianca and Mary Pat. Señor Carrots hops on top of the hay pile, squishing them all!

Chica Linda jumps in front of you and the PALs, stopping just before the barn doors, ready to take on whatever is making all this ruckus outside. You, Lucky, Pru, and Abigail are right behind her.

What could it be?

Turn to page 72 to find out!

Get Chica Linda and Boomerang to Help

"You've got this, Chica Linda. You're the strongest horse I know." Pru wraps her arms around Chica Linda's neck.

"Shine and save the day like the <u>knight you are</u>, Boomerang. CHARGE!" shouts Abigail.

The two horses run in unison and, with their back legs, kick at the door. They're strong enough that the door moves! They can see outside!

Turn to page 72 to find out what happens next!

Try the Battering Ram Again

"Why don't we give it one more shot? I think it moved a little last time; I really do!" says Lucky.

But even with all your might, the group can't get the door to open. Lucky sighs in frustration. "I guess my plan isn't going to work. Let's try someone else's idea!"

Go back to page 60 to try another idea.

Snips's Plan

"Lucky for you guys, I'm a genius," says Snips as he walks over to the corner of the stall. He's pretty proud of himself, and the twins are overcome by his confidence. Or Bianca is, in any case. This is Snips's moment to shine.

Snips turns around with five extra-tall shovels in hand.

"We're going to dig our way out all the way to <u>South America</u>, where there's no snow and we can be <u>free</u>. We'll finally get to start the town of Snipsadero, where everybody's gotta play with me whenever I want! It'll be perfect."

...

"Well? Whaddaya think?"

...

"There are plenty of places in South America that have snow. Like the Chilean mountains," Pru says.

"Snips, I don't think we're going to be able to dig our way out of the barn," Abigail says slowly, "much less all the way to South America."

"Plus, then we'll definitely be late for the party," Lucky adds.

Snips pouts. "You just don't understand how a genius's mind works. One day, I'll rule Snipsadero! If you ever figure a way out-"

Mary Pat steps forward. "If we're not digging our way out, then we should just sit and wait for a grown-up, even if it takes weeks! But don't worry. I have a board game to keep us from being <u>bored</u>. Get it?"

Use this board game to play checkers with your friends!

Turn to page 72 to find out what happens next!

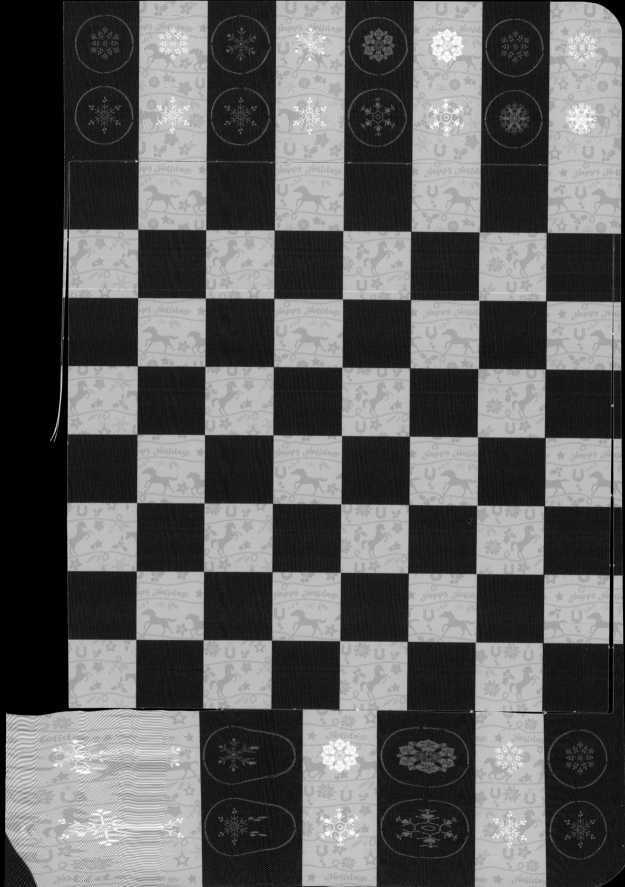

How to Play Checkers

1) Each player takes twelve checkers of the same color and places them on the dark squares of the first three rows on their side of the checkerboard.

2) You take your turn by moving one of your checkers. Checkers are always moved diagonally from one dark square to another open and neighboring dark square. Your pieces can only move in a forward direction unless they are "Kinged." If there are no free squares touching your checker, it cannot move.

3) If your opponent has a checker in a dark square neighboring one of your checkers with an empty square on the other side of it, you can use your piece to "jump" over them and remove their checker from the board. You can jump multiple checkers if they are lined up, BUT there must be empty spaces for you to land on between jumps.

4) If one of your checkers reaches the last row on the opposite side of the board, your piece will become a King. Place another checker on top of it. Now this checker can move forward <u>and</u> backward.

5) You win when your opponent has no more pieces on the board or can't move any of their pieces.

Pru's Plan Continued

Pru furrows her brow. Chica Linda neighs and nudges Pru's foot with her nose. That gives Pru an idea. She's going to get to that rooftop and save the day, no matter what.

"Lucky, get off Chica Linda's back!" Pru shouts. Lucky is confused, but slowly climbs down.

Pru gives a whistle and Chica Linda stands on her back legs, just as they have practiced, and a nudge from her nose gives Pru the push she needs to hoist herself to the roof. She's made it!

You lift the lantern up to Pru on the end of a shovel. When it reaches Pru's hand, she breathes a sigh of relief. You did it!

Now you just need someone to see her light.

Pru turns the lantern on and off, on and off, for what seems like forever, until she hears noise in the distance. It's growing louder and louder. Has someone finally come to get you all out of the snowed-in barn?

Turn to page 72 to find out!

Write Your Own Ending!

The plan worked!

Well...sort of. Chica Linda starts to sniff around the barn door. She senses something outside. It's Spirit! But he's not alone.

Who came to the rescue, just in time for the Winter Ball? Is it Al Granger and Jim, ready to plow the snow out of the way? Maybe Grayson had a change of heart and went out of his way to help the PALs?

In the space below, write how you and your new friends escape the barn and make it all the way to the inn for the party!

_____

_____

_____

_____

_____

_____

_____

_____

_____

_____

_____

_____

_____

At the Winter Ball

Girls! You made it. I'm so glad you can be here—_and_ with all these wonderful gifts—you're just in time for a winter miracle!

My dear brother Jim heard all about our train woes, and he brought the whole town together to help me bring my vision to life. So, with the help of Kate, Mr. Winthrop, all your parents, and even Fito and Estrella—I present to you Cora Prescott's Miradero Hot Cocoa Station, where all your hot cocoa wishes will come true.

First things first, here's how you make my grandmother's hot cocoa. It's a family secret, but after all your help, you've earned it! This recipe is simple and classic. It's the perfect base for all our town's recipes! _Cora_

Grandmother Prescott's
Hot Cocoa Recipe

What You'll Need:

- ½ cup of sugar
- ¼ cup of cocoa powder
- ¾ teaspoon of vanilla extract
- ⅓ cup of water
- 4 cups of milk

What to Do:

1) Combine the sugar, cocoa powder, vanilla extract, and water in a saucepan.
2) With an adult's help, heat the saucepan on the stove over medium heat. Stir until the ingredients become a syrup and it simmers.
3) Add the milk slowly while stirring.
4) Keep the mixture on the stove until the hot cocoa is your preferred temperature, then serve!

Now tell me what you're craving and we'll find just the right cocoa for you!

Hot Cocoa Flowchart

Are you looking for something traditional or a little different?

Traditional!

A little different...

Do you prefer to keep things sweet and simple, or fresh and exhilarating?

Sweet and simple

Fresh and exhilarating!

Try Salty and Sweet Hot Cocoa
Add 1 tablespoon of vanilla powder and ¼ teaspoon of sea salt to your cocoa powder before heating. Serve with whipped cream topped with a dash of sea salt!

Try Peppermint Hot Cocoa
Add 3 drops of peppermint extract to your prepared hot cocoa. Stir with a candy cane for a minty, sweet treat!

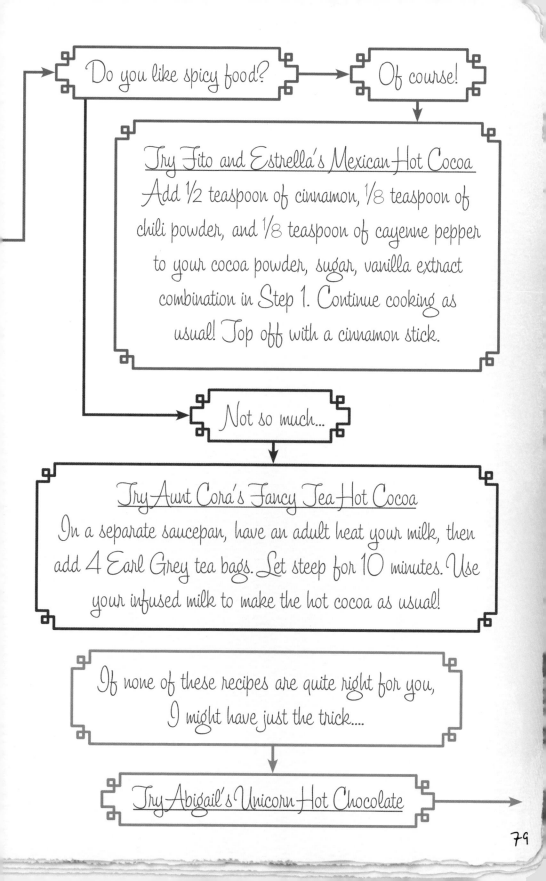

Do you like spicy food?

Of course!

__Try Fito and Estrella's Mexican Hot Cocoa__
Add ½ teaspoon of cinnamon, ⅛ teaspoon of chili powder, and ⅛ teaspoon of cayenne pepper to your cocoa powder, sugar, vanilla extract combination in Step 1. Continue cooking as usual! Top off with a cinnamon stick.

Not so much...

__Try Aunt Cora's Fancy Tea Hot Cocoa__
In a separate saucepan, have an adult heat your milk, then add 4 Earl Grey tea bags. Let steep for 10 minutes. Use your infused milk to make the hot cocoa as usual!

If none of these recipes are quite right for you, I might have just the trick....

__Try Abigail's Unicorn Hot Chocolate__

We're taking this one from the <u>top</u>. No cocoa here.

Abigail's Unicorn Hot Chocolate

What You'll Need:

- 1 cup of white chocolate chips
- 4 cups of milk
- 1 teaspoon of vanilla extract
- 1 teaspoon of strawberry syrup with extra for later
- Tons of whipped cream
- All the marshmallows
- So many sprinkles

What to Do:

1) With an adult's help, heat the white chocolate chips, milk, and vanilla extract in a saucepan over medium heat, stirring constantly.
2) Once the above is completely melted and combined, add a teaspoon of strawberry syrup so that your milk turns pink. If you want a stronger strawberry flavor, add a little more!
3) Serve your unicorn chocolate and top with whipped cream, marshmallows, sprinkles, and a drizzle of strawberry syrup!

This is the <u>best one</u>! It tastes like <u>magic</u>!

Part 5
Frontier Fillies' Guide to Winter

Fillies, gather!
Our herd leader, Ms. Hungerford, has put me in charge of Frontier Fillies Winter Preparedness Training. So, get in your adventuring gear, put that leaf hat on, and get ready for the best time <u>ever</u>!

As long as Snips doesn't wreck anything, that is.

Winter is one of the most fun times to be a Filly. Well, all year round is fun, but winter is <u>extra</u> fun. Maybe it's the winter camping, maybe it's licking icicles like they're ice pops, maybe it's the possibility of spotting the elusive yeti...

Abigail

Uh, Abigail...there's no such thing as— PRU

Are we ready, ladies and gentle-horses? LET'S GO! Abigail

I sure am. SNIPS

81

Winter Camping 101

Camping in the winter can be really tricky, so the best thing we can do is what Frontier Fillies always do: be prepared.

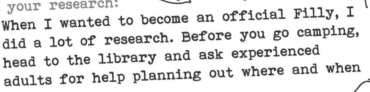

Do your research:
When I wanted to become an official Filly, I did a lot of research. Before you go camping, head to the library and ask experienced adults for help planning out where and when to go.

Always go with experienced adult campers!
My dad and Mr. Prescott are always helpful, even if they sometimes go a little overboard with preparations.

Use the right kind of shelter:
If you're camping in a tent instead of a cabin, make sure your tent is meant for winter. The right tent will keep you warm and help you withstand lower temperatures and unexpected weather. Same goes for sleeping bags—a winter sleeping bag will keep you extra toasty!

Lay down waterproof tarps beneath your tent, and blankets below your sleeping bag,:
Keeping your sleeping bag dry and warm is the trick to keeping you dry and warm all through the night!

Pack layers!
No one wants frozen toes or fingers or ears or <u>anything</u>, for that matter.

And the oldest rule in the books...

<u>KEEP YOUR BOOTS DRY!</u>

Campfire Snacks

Now that you're all comfy by the campfire, it's time for the best part of camping: <u>snacks</u>. Boomerang and I love snuggling with a cinnamon roll and some apples by the campfire, don't we, boy?

Campfire Orange-Baked Cinnamon Rolls

What You'll Need:

> 1 can of cinnamon roll dough
> Aluminum foil
>
> Icing
> Oranges

What to Do:

1) Have an adult slice off the top of an orange and put it to the side.
2) Scoop out the juicy inside of the orange.
3) Place a roll of cinnamon roll dough inside the scooped-out orange.
4) Replace the top of the orange and wrap the whole thing in foil.
5) Have an adult carefully place it inside the campfire for 15 minutes. You can put it right on the coals!
6) Remove the cinnamon roll from the fire and discard the foil and top of the orange. Now you can top it with icing, cool, and enjoy directly from the peel!

Campfire Pranks

Snacks are good and all, but pranks are better! These Fillies need some excitement, and Snips and Señor Carrots are here to help! They'll thank me for it later. SQUEAK SQUEAK!

Pinecone Mice
(for scaring big sisters named Abigail)

What You'll Need:

Pinecones
Hot glue gun
Cardboard
Twine

Acorns
Permanent marker
Scissors
Ribbon or fleece

What to Do:

1) Start by having an adult help you carefully cut off the top of a pinecone.

2) With an adult's help, use your hot glue gun to glue the flat end of an acorn to the cut end of the pinecone. Use the permanent marker to draw on the eyes!

3) With your adult, use your scissors to cut out long feet, little paws, and big round ears for your mouse from the cardboard.

4) Glue them onto the pinecone!
5) Tie a piece of twine to the bottom of the pinecone to make your mouse's squiggly tail.
6) Now put them in your sister's tent and wait for her to run out SCREAMING IN TERROR!

It's cold out there. Maybe you can give your mouse a scarf made out of ribbon or fleece. <u>But don't make it too cute.</u>

Aw, this mouse is so cute! And snuggly. Look at the little scarf! Do you think Boomerang would like it?

Dang it! Why'd ya have to go and ruin all my fun, Abigail?

Just look at how adorable it is, Snips! I shall name him Cinnamon Roll, so he reminds Boomerang of our campfire nights.
Oh! I can also wrap some twine around the middle of the mouse and use it to tie him like an ornament. Wouldn't that be nice, Boomerang?

...Señor Carrots would like that, too. We'll name ours Pranksy.

Badges

Wow, PAL! You're a real Frontier Filly, you know that? Check out these wintertime badges you earned!

Winter Riding Badge

You've learned how to take care of your horse in the cold and have successfully ridden snowy trails and stayed safe while avoiding wintry obstacles!

Winter Camping Badge

You've done all your research and now know exactly how to stay warm and dry when you're sleeping outdoors throughout the winter.

Winter Cookout Badge

You've safely prepared yummy and gooey snacks that are perfect for sharing around a campfire with your best PALs.

Prank Badge

You've pranked your sister or friends with some cute—uh, TERRIFYING—crafts!

Draw Your Own Badges

What other Frontier Filly badges
can you earn? Draw them here!

Winter Fill-In

It was a(n) _____ winter's day. Lucky,
(adjective)

Pru, and Abigail were _____ through the
(verb ending in –ING)

Miradero canyons. There was _____,
(adjective)

_____ snow on the ground. The PALs
(color)

were enjoying a quick ride before heading back to

Lucky's house, where Kate was treating them to a

candy and _____ night.
(activity)

With _____ in the lead, Spirit
(Pru, Lucky, or Abigail)

skidded to a stop. "What's wrong, boy?" asked Lucky.

She _____ him comfortingly. But Spirit
(past tense verb)

still had a(n) _____ look on his face
(adjective)

as he stared due _____.
(cardinal direction)

Then, like a(n) _____, Spirit took off
(noun)

galloping! Lucky held on tight. What did Spirit hear?

When Spirit finally slowed at a clearing, the PALs

found a campsite. There was half-eaten _____
(type of candy)

everywhere! It was a(n) _____.
(noun)

"Do you think it was a(n) _____?"
(animal)

Pru asked _____.
(adverb)

"Do you think it was Butch LePray?" Lucky asked

_____.
(adverb)

"Do you think it was a(n) _____?"
(mythical creature)

offered Abigail with excitement.

Abigail slid from Boomerang's saddle to the

ground and examined a(n) _____ more
(noun)

closely. "Uh-oh. These tracks look like they're from

a(n) _____! RUN!"
(different mythical creature)

Lucky and Pru looked directly at each other and

_____.
(past tense verb)

"Why aren't you panicking?" Abigail was jumping

like a(n) _____.
(animal)

Pru and Lucky both grabbed Abigail's shoulders

to calm her down. With a deep breath, Lucky put on

her best Boxcar Bonnie voice and pointed out the

evidence: _____, _____,
(noun)   (noun)

and _____. It couldn't be a(n)
(noun)

_____ who created this mess! It had
(previous mythical creature)

to be a smaller creature.

After _____ minutes staring at all
(number)

the evidence, Abigail's face lit up! She knew exactly

what happened:

"SNIPS! You ate all our candy for tonight!"

From behind a(n) _____ Snips crawled
(noun)

out with a grin on his _____.
(noun)

"What?" he asked. "If Teacher didn't want me

to take all the candy from her bowl, sneak to my campsite, and eat all the food in my hideout, THEN WHY DID SHE LEAVE THE BOWL OUT?"

As Snips wobbled over to Señor Carrots, face covered in _____, he started to turn

(same type of candy)

_____!

(color)

"Uh-oh, looks like someone had too much candy!"

Farewell For Now!

Well, friend, I hope you enjoyed your time in Miradero! Winter is so special, and I know that my and Spirit's winters were extra special this year because of you! We hope that you stay warm and spend plenty of time with your favorite horses and best PALs this winter. Come back and see us soon!

Your PALs Forever,

Pru, Lucky, and Abigail

Glossary

Battering ram: A heavy object swung or rammed against a door to break it down

Blacksmith: A person who handmakes or repairs iron things

Bran mash: A food for horses made with bran and hot water

Dressage: The art of riding and training a horse in a manner that develops obedience, flexibility, and balance

Foal: A young horse

Frontier: The land outside a developed territory

Gelding: A castrated (neutered) male horse

Graze: To eat grass in a field

Herd: A large group of animals that live, feed, or migrate together

Molasses: A sweet syrup that is separated from sugar in manufacturing

Mustang: An American wild horse

Pinto: A horse that has irregular patches of white and another color

Ramada: A fenced ring in which a person can ride

Sleigh: A sled drawn by horses

Stable: A building used for keeping horses

Stall: An individual compartment for an animal in a stable

Stallion: An uncastrated adult male horse

Steed: A horse available for riding

Trick riding: The act of performing stunts while riding a horse, such as standing on a galloping horse